SHOWER LAND

FEEL THE FREEZE

BOOKS BY NAT AMOORE

Secrets of a Schoolyard Millionaire

The Power of Positive Pranking

The Right Way to Rock

We Run Tomorrow

Shower Land: Break the Curse

Shower Land: Feel the Freeze

Shower Land: Walk the Plank (September 2024)

SHOWER LAND

FEEL THE FREEZE

NAT AMOORE

JAMES HART

PUFFIN BOOKS

UK | USA | Canada | Ireland | Australia
India | New Zealand | South Africa | China

Penguin
Random House
Australia

Penguin Random House Australia is part of the Penguin Random House group of companies whose addresses can be found at global.penguinrandomhouse.com.

First published by Puffin Books, an imprint of
Penguin Random House Australia Pty Ltd, in 2024

Cover design by Rebecca King © Penguin Random House Australia Pty Ltd
Internal design and typesetting by Midland Typesetters, Australia

Printed and bound in Australia by Griffin Press, an accredited
ISO AS/NZS 14001 Environmental Management Systems printer

NATIONAL LIBRARY OF AUSTRALIA

A catalogue record for this book is available from the National Library of Australia

FSC www.fsc.org MIX Paper | Supporting responsible forestry FSC® C018684

ISBN 978 1 76134 253 0

penguin.com.au

We at Penguin Random House Australia acknowledge that Aboriginal and Torres Strait Islander peoples are the Traditional Custodians and the first storytellers of the lands on which we live and work. We honour Aboriginal and Torres Strait Islander peoples' continuous connection to Country, waters, skies and communities. We celebrate Aboriginal and Torres Strait Islander stories, traditions and living cultures; and we pay our respects to Elders past and present.

To Nikki,

for being by my side through it all.

When I need someone, you are my Frivlig.

Chapter 1

Zombie's armpit

'Daaaaaaaaad! Felix's hair smells like feet!'

Olly leant away from Felix. He pinched his nose and waved his hand dramatically.

'Shut your trap!' Felix whispered through gritted teeth. 'It's not that bad.'

But it was.

Felix hadn't had a shower in **two weeks**. His fingernails had collected a dark greenish scum, stray cats had started to follow him and he may or may not have seen something move in his hair yesterday. He was ***really*** hoping it was just his imagination.

Felix knew he couldn't keep it up for much longer, but the thought of stepping into the shower and disappearing to who-knows-where terrified him.

Olly pointed at his brother. 'Smell him, Dad. **SMELL HIM!**'

Dad was busy preparing some generously slathered peanut butter sandwiches and glanced up briefly. 'I'm not going to **smell** him, Olly.'

Felix breathed a sigh of relief. He'd been keeping his distance from Dad for the last week hoping to avoid the usual 'check behind the ears' routine. So far, Dad had been super busy with work, and he'd gotten away with it. School was a bit trickier, but today they had a class excursion to the zoo and Felix was hoping his new scent would simply blend in there.

But Olly just wouldn't let it go. 'You really should, Dad. It's **bad**. He smells like a wet dog rolled in blue cheese.'

Felix glared at his brother. 'Quit it!'

Olly didn't quit it. 'He's like silent but deadly's evil twin. We could bottle it and called the fragrance "Zombie's Armpit". Welcome to **Stinktown**, population, that guy!' He pointed at Felix and held his nose tight.

'All right, slightly overdramatic perhaps, Olly?' Dad shook his head. 'It can't be that bad, he showers every morning.'

Felix focused on the Rice Bubbles floating around in his bowl, as he tried to capture them with his spoon.

'Nah-ah!' Olly stated triumphantly. 'He just goes in there, turns on the water and sits on the toilet reading his *K-Zone* magazines.'

Felix turned on Olly and growled. 'Are you spying on me? In the bathroom?'

Olly grinned triumphantly. '**See!** He admits it.'

Felix winced, realising the mistake he'd made. He turned to his dad, who was staring straight at him, brow furrowed.

'It has been a while since I got a hug,' Dad said, head tilting to the side. He slowly put down the peanut butter-covered knife. 'Come here.'

Felix forced a smile. 'Dad, c'mon, you know Olly is just goofing around.'

Dad didn't move. 'Come. Here.'

Felix reluctantly got up from the table and walked towards the kitchen as Olly chanted: 'Smell him, smell him, smell him!' Felix stopped at the end of the bench, wondering how much he could get for his little brother on eBay.

'Here!' Dad said and pointed to the spot directly in front of him.

Felix hung his head and approached his father.

Dad looked at Felix's hair and his eyes widened. He took a deep sniff and turned a pale shade of green. He grabbed Felix's hand and inspected his filthy nails.

'**Felix Anthony McKillop**, when was the last time you showered?'

Felix stared at his grubby feet, not wanting to make eye contact with his dad. He knew that voice. It was the voice Dad used when he was trying to be an

understanding and supportive parent, but what he really wanted to do was string his kids from the ceiling fan and turn it up to five.

'Thirteen days ago!' Olly announced proudly.

Felix glared at him. Seriously, ***zero*** privacy when you have a younger sibling.

'That's it!' Dad placed his hand on Felix's back and pushed him towards the bathroom. '**Shower now**. You will wash every last square centimetre of yourself, even if I have to watch you!'

Felix headed to his room.

'Where do you think you're going?' Dad asked.

'To get my towel! I can at least get a towel, right?'

'Don't get smart with me,' Dad warned. 'What made you think you could go ***thirteen*** days without a shower? What were you thinking? Is this some kind of protest?'

Felix paused, hand on towel. 'Yes,' he said, turning slowly. 'A protest.'

He knew his dad was super passionate about the environment, protecting animals, reducing waste and conserving energy and ... **water!**

'I'm trying to save water,' Felix announced. 'You know, every drop counts and all.'

Dad considered this, nodding thoughtfully. 'Fair enough,' he finally said.

Felix felt a giant teleportation-sized weight lift off his shoulders. No shower and no getting **zapped** to another world.

'I appreciate and respect your environmental stance,' Dad said earnestly. 'So here's how you can contribute to the cause AND smell less like a dirty gym sock ... no more playing in the sprinkler on the weekend *and* you and Olly hand-water the garden with the grey water.'

'Whaaaaaat!?' Olly cried from the kitchen. 'How am I getting punished for having a stinky brother?'

'Dad –' Felix started.

'Shower. Now.'

Felix knew better than to argue when his dad's eyebrows were so frowny that they almost touched. He grabbed his towel and a pair of speedos in case his dad was serious about watching him.

Felix reluctantly walked into the bathroom. His dad followed, closing the toilet seat and perching on top. He opened one of his *Vogue* magazines and settled in.

'Are you really going to **watch me?**' Felix protested.

'Pull the shower curtain shut, but I'm going to make sure that you stay in there AND that you're clean when you get out. No son of mine is going around with hair that smells like **Shrek's gumboot!**'

Felix groaned and stepped into the shower. He pulled the curtain across and stripped down. After flinging his clothing

piece by piece over the shower rail, he was finally left holding the speedos.

He looked around the very normal shower. It was going to be fine. It was probably all just in his imagination anyway. There was no such thing as a teleporting shower. It was **ridiculous**. He'd probably slipped in the shower and hit his head and imagined it all.

Felix conveniently ignored the part of his brain that tried to remind him about the **medieval outfit** he'd disposed of in the school bin.

The whole thing was just a bad dream. For sure. Now he was going to have a perfectly normal shower . . . that didn't send him anywhere. A shower that did nothing except scare away the small creature living in his hair . . . and leave him smelling like cherry blossom (according to the soap label).

Yep, that's what was going to happen.

That and **only that**.

But Felix slipped into his speedos . . . just in case.

'I don't hear the water running!' Dad shouted from the other side of the shower curtain. 'No shower, no zoo trip!'

Felix did **NOT** want to miss the zoo trip. He had been looking forward to it for ages.

It was going to be okay. It was just a shower.

He reached up slowly and placed his hand on the tap. Looking up at the silver showerhead that loomed over him, he took a deep breath and turned. The water hit his head and . . .

REEEEKKKKKK!

There was a sound like rusty brakes on a metro train, a blinding flash of white light and the strong smell of singed hair.

Not again!

Felix's eyes tried to adjust to his surroundings, but the white light seemed to remain. A burning sensation prickled at his feet. He rubbed his eyes and looked again. Everything was still white. His entire body shuddered and his teeth chattered. He looked down at his burning feet. He was **standing in snow!** That burning sensation was actually freezing. When something is so cold it's hot, that's bad.

Felix lifted his head, peering through the white surrounding him. It wasn't the light, it was snow.

Everywhere.

Felix wrapped his arms around his shivering body and while he was glad to be wearing speedos, he knew they would help very little in this climate. Worried his toes might **drop off**, he hopped up onto a fallen tree to get his feet out of the ice.

His teeth banged against each other like a jackhammer. He tried to think warm thoughts like when he peed in his wetsuit while surfing in winter. But it didn't work.

Felix couldn't feel his toes, his lips had gone numb and his body was shaking uncontrollably. This was it. This was the end. Dad's need for clean hair was going to lead to **Felix's tragic end**. His head began to spin. He couldn't feel his limbs and his legs felt like they were going to give way.

Screeeeeekkkk!

Felix heard a loud scraping sound from behind. Every part of him wanted to turn around to see what it was, but his body wouldn't respond. Should he be scared? Probably. But he was too cold to feel fear. He couldn't feel **anything**. He was numb from top to toe.

A dark shadow loomed over him. Or maybe he was hallucinating. It was hard to tell. The cold was too much and Felix knew he was about to pass out. But then his freezing body was suddenly surrounded by fur. Strong arms caught him just before he lost consciousness, and everything went **black**.

Chapter 2

Pants!

Felix was slowly aware of a crackling sound in the distance. His tummy rumbled at the delicious smell of cooking stew. And most importantly, he could feel his limbs. He tried to drag his mind back into the world but it was like swimming through quicksand. He forced his eyes open, but all he could see was flickering orange. **Panic** rose in his chest. The last time he'd seen that was when Dad left the cardboard packaging on the frozen lasagne in the oven and it had caught on fire. Was Dad trying to cook outside his expertise again?

Felix sat up too quickly and he got that roller-coaster feeling where it takes a second for your insides to catch up with your body. His eyes adjusted and focused on an open fire in front of him. The warmth that came from it was like a **big bear hug** from Grandma (minus the vanilla smell and the endless supply of

Anzac bickies). He was lying on a leather sleeping mat with a large fur spread across his lap. Logs of wood formed the walls of the small hut he was in. It was cosy and smelt like one of those little pine trees Dad hung in his car. Next to the fire was a stove holding a pot that bubbled away softly. Felix guessed that's where the delicious smell was coming from. Strange instruments, or maybe weapons, hung near the entrance and a single door at the back led into what looked like a bedroom.

He ran his hands over his body. **Clothes!** Someone had dressed him. Thank goodness he wasn't rocking those red speedos anymore. And this time he hadn't even had to steal anything. A pelt poncho covered his chest. Underneath that, a cream thermal. Felix lifted the fur blanket – **pants!** Brown leather ones at that. Hooley dooley, was he happy to be wearing pants. And no wonder his toes felt so snuggly – his feet had been covered in sheepskin-lined slipper-boots. Felix felt a little like that time he'd dressed as a Viking for Book Week. And he didn't hate it.

Felix shuffled closer to the fire and rubbed his hands in front of its flame. Through the window he could see the snow whipping against the glass. He didn't know where he was but he was sure glad he wasn't still out there, standing around in his swimmers, shaking like Olly on red cordial.

'He wakes!'

A voice boomed from behind Felix. He jumped to his feet and spun around to face an enormous man with a beard that looked like someone had stapled an entire German shepherd to his face. He was twice as tall as Felix and about six times as wide. Fingers crossed he was friendly because getting past him would be like trying to take on a brick wall with a paddle-pop stick.

Felix searched his very empty brain for something to say. He needed a formal greeting that expressed both gratitude for saving his life and also implied that

he hoped it wasn't just saved to then be ended. After a few seconds of silence, he landed on, 'Hi.'

The man's face crinkled in confusion. He then raised his hand in a sort of salute and said, 'Salutations?' His deep voice filled the hut and bounced off the walls.

If Felix had learnt anything in his travels (which now consisted of **two whole teleportations** to other worlds via his highly unpredictable shower) it was: 'Go with the flow'.

He raised his hand, copying the man and said, 'Salutations.'

A huge grin spread across his bearded face. 'You speak Angla? Are you being hungry?'

Felix glanced at the pot on the stove. The smell made his mouth water and there was no way he was saying no. He hadn't had a chance to finish his breakfast and whatever **that** was, it smelt way better than soggy Rice Bubbles.

'Yes, please. And thank you,' he said as politely as he could.

The man turned over his shoulder and yelled towards the door. '**Torkal!** He be awake. Let's eating.'

A small boy stuck his head around the doorframe and looked Felix up and down. He was probably about Olly's age but a bit taller. As the large man began to move around the hut setting up for dinner, the boy slowly came out. He was dressed similarly to Felix and approached carefully, not blinking the entire time.

'You be friendly?' he asked, tilting his head to the side and narrowing his eyes.

Felix smiled. Olly eyed him with the same suspicion anytime he tried to do anything nice. Which to be fair, wasn't very often.

'I am.' Felix nodded. 'Very friendly.'

The boy seemed satisfied, taking him at his word. 'Very well. **We eat**.'

Chapter
3

Fearlax

They sat around a small wooden table on chairs carved from tree trunks. Steam rose from their bowls of stew. In the centre of the table was freshly baked bread, a slab of golden butter and a bowl of roasted chestnuts. It took every bit of self-control from Felix not to dive in immediately. But he tried to remember his dad's wise words: *You can eat like a hyena when you're at home, but* ***pleeeeeease*** *use some manners at other people's houses.*

Felix sat up straight and kept his elbows off the table.

The boy put his hand on his chest. 'I be Torkal.' He reached for the man's chest. 'This be my father, Norg. You?'

Felix put a hand on his own chest. 'Felix,' he said confidently.

Torkal and Norg looked at each other and smirked.

'What?' Felix asked.

'We have the word **Fearlax** in our tongue. It be the spirit to protect us from the enemy.'

'The enemy?'

'Anything that bother us. We even put a Fearlax in the fields to scare away the pests,' explained Torkal.

Felix furrowed his brow. 'Like a **scarecrow?**'

The father and son looked confused. Felix stood up, raised his arms to the side and hung his head, doing his best scarecrow impression. It wasn't going to win him any Oscars.

Torkal scoffed. 'Your Fearlax look like it be sleeping.' He stood up and put his hands up to the sides of his head, fingers

splayed like antlers. Then he made a scary face and growled.

'Yas!' Norg shouted, pointing excitedly. **'This be a Fearlax!'**

Felix decided he would try to get through this adventure without encountering one of those. His tummy grumbled and he shovelled a heaped spoon of delicious stew into his mouth. It was getting dark outside and the time difference was a little odd, but the stew was so yum that he didn't mind eating it for breakfast. 'Do you two live here alone?'

Torkal shook his head, still chewing. 'Nay. Mother be out guarding.'

Outside the thick window, the snow seemed to stretch forever. He'd never been in the mountains before, but he imagined there might very well be some **dangerous animals**. Foxes, angry deer, maybe even a bear or two.

'Guarding from what?' he asked, cramming in another spoonful of stew.

Torkal didn't miss a beat. **'Yeti.'**

Felix almost spat his food out. Coughing and spluttering, he checked that he'd heard correctly. 'Did you say **yeti?**'

'Yas,' confirmed Norg. 'You have yeti problem too, no? Being from other tri-villages?'

Felix felt that familiar feeling creep in. The realisation that he was in another place, another time, another world he **didn't understand**. Where surprises lurked around every corner and apparently things that didn't exist in Cork Bay were just as common as bin chickens. Dragons and witches' curses weren't great, but **yetis definitely sounded worse**.

'Stealing our animals be bad, but taking the children be truly terrible.'

Felix's eyes widened. Yep, yetis were definitely worse. **'Taking children?'**

Torkal and Norg both dropped their heads. 'Sixteen so far,' whispered Torkal.

Felix had so many questions, but the sadness in their eyes stopped him from asking. Based on intel gathered in his last shower-teleporting mission, Felix assumed he would have to solve another problem to get home. He just hoped deep down in the gurgly part of his tummy that the problem was **not** stopping a ferocious yeti. He wasn't sure he could take on a yeti and save sixteen children. Yeti fighting wasn't really his strong point. Maybe there was a little veggie garden that needed attention instead. Felix was **great** with cherry tomatoes.

Chapter 4

Wilding without clothing

BOOM!

The door burst open, breaking the silence and scaring the bejeebers out of Felix. A cold wind whipped into the hut, bringing with it a swirl of snow that nipped the end of his nose and stung his eyes.

As the icy wind settled, it revealed a huge silhouette that filled the doorway entirely. Felix rubbed his eyes. Leather armour covered the figure and a huge axe was strapped to her back.

'Mama!' Torkal cried and jumped to his feet, running to the woman and wrapping his arms around her leg.

'Salut, my boy,' she said gently, scooping him up into her arms.

Torkal was a decent sized eight-year-old but his mum picked him up like he was a newborn puppy. She was so strong that it appeared her muscles had invited some other muscles over to play.

Her gaze settled on Felix. 'Ah, our little **ice boy**. You be awake?' She grinned at him teasingly.

Felix nodded and mumbled, 'Hi,' then shook his head and corrected himself. Raising his hand like Norg had done, he said (not so confidently), 'Salutations?'

The woman laughed. A laugh that bounced around the hut and filled it with even more warmth than the fire. 'Does that be a question?' she said with a cheeky smile.

Felix grinned back. He couldn't help it. There was something about her that made him feel safe and comfortable. Like a human sleeping bag. 'I'm Felix,' he said, stepping towards her and into the light from the fire.

'I be Bodil,' she said, and then stopped. The smile dropped from her face and she turned pale.

Felix froze. Had he done something wrong? Said something wrong? It was hard to pick up on new customs every time he had a shower. Had he offended her?

'Is that . . . ?' Her eyes scanned slowly over Felix's outfit.

Norg stepped forward, putting a hand gently on her shoulder. 'It be the only clothes we had that be fitting him. He needed warming.'

Bodil looked at him with wet eyes and nodded. She pushed a smile back onto her face. 'Of course. From ours to yours, Felix.' She put Torkal down and extended her hand to Felix. When he put his hand in hers, it disappeared like a gummy bear being **swallowed by a hippo**. She smiled at him and Felix couldn't help but feel warm. She smelt like pine needles, and even though she looked so strong, the act of shaking hands was as gentle as a hug.

She stood back up. 'Now which of the tri-villages be you from so we can be returning you home. And finding out why they left you wilding without clothing.'

BA-BA-DAAAAAAAA!

A trumpeting sound pierced the night air, drawing the family's attention to the sky.

'Your story shall have to wait,' announced Norg. 'The tri-villagers assembly be now. You come with us, Felix. Maybe your family be there.'

Felix doubted that very much. His family were most likely eating Rice

Bubbles and reading *Vogue*. But *this* family made him feel safe and he was more than happy to stick with them until he worked out how to get home.

'Maybe tonight be the night?' Torkal said. 'I feel it be.'

Bodil ruffled his hair. 'I hope so.' She turned to Norg. 'Maybe tonight I **raise my hand**.'

Norg shook his head. 'No. Torkal still be here. We agreed.'

Bodil hugged her son tight. 'We go now.'

The family prepared to leave the hut. They gathered and packed shoulder bags and put on extra clothing.

Felix stared longingly at the stew he hadn't finished and the chestnuts he hadn't had a chance to try. He didn't want to see them go to waste, so he grabbed a couple and popped them in his pocket for later.

'You need more warming,' announced Norg and added another layer of fur to Felix. He was given boots and gloves, a jacket and a hat from the cupboard.

The whole family fell silent as they watched him dress and the quiet made Felix uneasy. But before he had time to ask questions, Bodil shuffled the family out the door and into the **freezing night**.

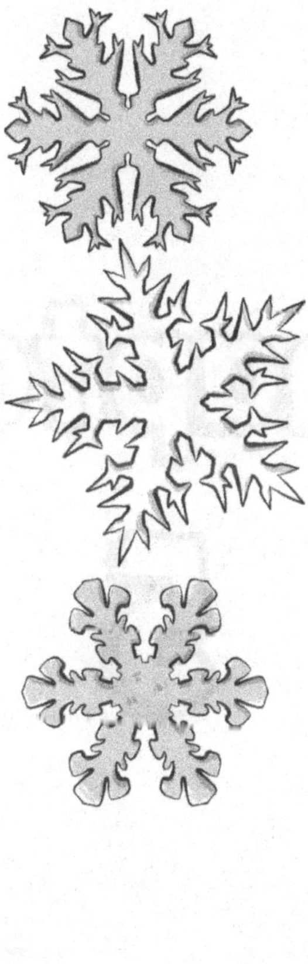

Chapter 5

Eaten by a yeti

Light snow whipped around Felix's face. He and Torkal huddled together, following close behind the adults and using them as a wind block. As Felix hugged himself tightly, he felt very grateful for the fur jacket he wore and the warm clothes he'd been given. Had he even said thank you? World jumping did **terrible** things to his manners.

They passed hut after hut, glowing firelight coming from within. Many of the houses appeared run-down, with holes in the roofs that needed patching or fixing. Felix didn't know a lot about living in the cold, but not having **holes in your house** seemed like a logical first step.

He pointed out one house to Torkal. 'Why don't they fix their house?'

'The wood we be using for our homes comes from the forest on top of the mountain. Thick trees. Down the bottom be just for firewood.'

'So why don't you get the mountain wood?'

Torkal looked at Felix like he knew nothing. Which to be fair, is **exactly** how much he knew. 'The yeti be on mountain. No wood for us while yeti lives there.'

They continued to pass more houses. In the front yard of one house stood a snowman. But it wasn't a cute, Olaf-style snowman. It was a giant, **scary creature** made of ice, with huge icicle fangs and red berries for eyes. Poked into its head were two giant branches, giving the impression of antlers.

Felix nudged Torkal. 'What is that?'

Torkal smiled. 'That be a **Fearlax**.'

Felix was a little offended.

'We build them to keep the yeti away from our homes. Away from the children.'

Torkal scoffed. 'They don't be working.'

Next, they passed an open area with a playground built in the middle. A slide made entirely of ice was the centrepiece. Felix's butt felt cold just thinking about it. He and every other kid in Cork Bay had

burnt their bums on the park slide. After a summer's day of roasting in the sun, a hot slide was a common danger. But he wasn't sure an **ice slide** would be any kinder on a delicate tush.

Felix put his head down and watched as his feet fell into the footprints left in the snow by Bodil. They were huge and made his boot look tiny inside. When Olly was three, he'd put on Dad's work boots and stumbled around the house. Dad and Felix rolled on the ground laughing as he'd struggled like some **uncoordinated clown-baby**. The familiar stab of homesickness hit Felix. Although it wasn't as bad as before. It was mixed up with a bit of excitement at the **adventure**.

A small part of him worried that he might not get home this time. But he pushed that feeling down into his fur boots and told himself to follow the plan.

Find the problem, then find the solution, then **KAZAM!** He'd be back faster than you can say 'beware of teleporting showers'…

They passed another Fearlax.

…If he didn't get **eaten by a yeti** first.

A cold wind whipped around the foursome. The family all instinctively put a hand to their heads, holding their hats down. But Felix was too slow. The wind lifted his fur cap and tossed it around in the air. He chased it like a kitten swiping at a torchlight until it fell to the ground.

Bending down to pick it up, Felix saw a name stitched into the inner brim.

STEN.

Felix quickly put the hat on before his ears froze off. He ran to join the family and they continued walking.

'Torkal?'

'Yas?'

Felix kicked at the snow on the ground. 'Who is Sten?'

Torkal stopped and looked up at his parents, but they couldn't hear the conversation over the wind and the woollen hats strapped over their ears. He continued walking but kept his voice low.

'He be my **brother**.'

Felix tried to ask the next question as carefully as he could. 'Did he get taken? By the . . . yeti?'

Torkal nodded.

Felix thought about his brother. Olly was a **pain in the butt**. No question about that. He used Felix's stuff without asking and ate all Felix's Tiny Teddys (even though Olly asked Dad to get him Pizza Shapes). He always left his Lego lying where Felix could step on it AND sometimes even used Felix's toothbrush, which was just **downright gross**. But despite all that, Felix would still hate it if Olly was eaten by a yeti.

'How long has he been missing?' Felix asked.

'Ten days, four hours and . . .' Torkal looked at the sky, his gaze following from the moon to the stars and back. '. . . thirty-seven minutes.'

'I'm sorry.'

Torkal grinned. 'Don't be.'

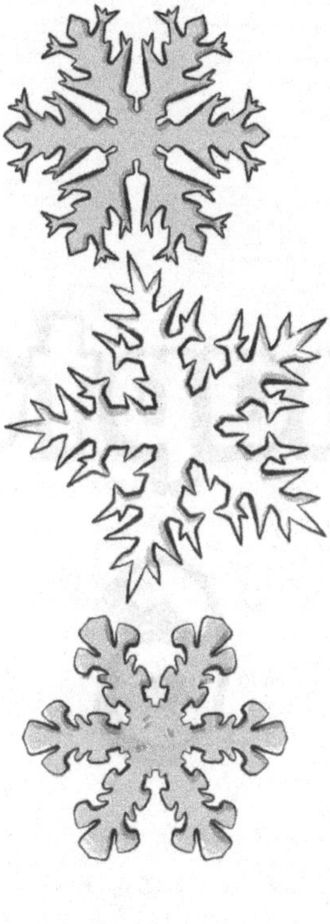

Chapter 6

Rising

Felix was shocked. Brothers could be hard work, but that seemed a little cold, even for a younger brother. 'Okaaaaaaaay.'

Torkal grabbed his arm. 'No, I do not …' he laughed. 'I mean, he still be **alive**.'

'How do you know?' asked Felix.

'The **animals** told me.'

If yetis and yeti-napped kids and speedos in the snow weren't enough to confuse Felix, then this kid was certainly going to do the job.

'I sent a hare to check on him,' Torkal continued, 'and he be telling me the children still be alive.'

Felix stopped in his tracks. 'I'm sorry ... **What?** You said a whole bunch of things there and I didn't get any of them.'

'*Ahhhh*.' Torkal bowed his head in sympathy. 'You must be from the Bears? I heard your clan do not have **Risings**.'

Felix had had enough. 'Okay. Here's what we are going to do. Imagine I'm

from a whole other world. Imagine I've just been dropped here, in the middle of the snow, with **no clue** how things work in your world. Imagine, if you can, that I don't even know what a Rising is, and that where I come from, people don't talk to hares and while we do have to worry about a possum dying under the house and stinking up the floorboards, we definitely do **NOT** have to worry about our siblings getting stolen by yetis. Can you imagine **all that?**'

Torkal blinked slowly. 'Not really.'

Felix groaned.

'But I can try.'

'Thank you.' Felix rubbed his eyes to get the snow off his eyelashes. 'Now explain everything.'

'Some children of the Fox have a Rising. A special power. It stays with them until they turn thirteen, then they lose it and forget they ever had it. Children talk not of the Rising to the adults. They don't understand. They don't remember.'

Felix thought about how his dad totally didn't remember what it was like to be a kid. How he didn't understand why it was more fun to eat ice cream straight out of the tub than put it in a bowl. How he didn't understand that the appropriate Milo ratio was 7/8 of the cup Milo and a dribble of milk. So it made sense. You know, if those things were all **really cool superpowers**.

'Okay. And you have a Rising?' Felix asked.

'Yas.' Torkal didn't seem like he was going to elaborate.

Felix continued walking, his boots pressing marks into the snow. He wasn't a big fan of the cold here, but he could definitely handle hanging out in a place where kids get superpowers. 'Soooooo? What is it? Can you leap tall buildings in a single bound?'

'What be a **building?**'

Felix laughed. 'What is your Rising?'

Torkal beamed proudly. 'I can talk to animals.'

'Ooooohhh, riiiiiight!' Felix smiled. 'Well, that certainly makes the whole "I talked to a rabbit" thing a little clearer.'

'It be an arctic hare and I sent it up the mountain to spy on the yeti. He told me all the children still be alive. Including Sten. We just have to get them back.'

'But how?'

'This I do not know. I want to go but they won't let me.' Torkal nodded towards his parents.

'Makes sense,' Felix pointed out. 'They've already lost one kid to the yeti.'

'I guess so,' said Torkal. 'But someone has to **help them**.'

They walked in silence. Torkal's parents checked over their shoulder every now and then to make sure the children were still following.

Despite all the layers, Felix was starting to become a **human iceblock** again. He shoved his hands deep into his pockets and thought warm thoughts. Steamy asphalt in Cork Bay in summer.

Him and Olly trying to get to the beach without shoes and almost leaving the soles of their feet behind, melted in the lava-hot road.

'I have a brother,' Felix said quietly.

Torkal looked up. 'What's his name?'

'Olly.' As Felix said his name a pang of missing hit him. He wasn't usually the sentimental type, but right now he'd love to give Olly a hug.

'Is he nice? Your brother?' Torkal asked.

Felix laughed. 'Not really. He's actually a bit of a brat. But **I love him**.'

Torkal smiled. 'Same. Sten and I fought all the time. But he be my brother. Always.'

Felix could hear a sizzling and crackling sound. As they rounded the corner, he saw a huge bonfire blazing in the middle of a clearing. The fire was in a triangular pit. At the three corners of the triangle sat a group of people, each with a pole holding a giant coat of arms.

One had a **bear**, another a **snow leopard** and the last a **fox**. He followed the family towards the group with the fox flag and joined their huddle.

'Can you see your family?' Norg asked. 'Are you Bear or Leopard?'

Felix didn't know how to explain that his family were probably more likely **seagull** or **blowfly** and there was a pretty good chance they weren't at this meeting. Dad didn't even like walking on the kitchen tiles without his ugg boots on. He wasn't likely to join a meeting in the middle of the snowy mountains after dark.

'I don't think my family are here,' Felix said, avoiding a direct answer.

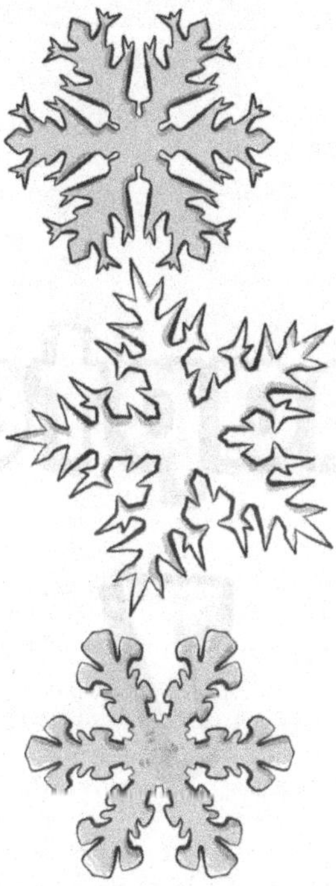

Chapter 7

What's a Frivlig?

Bodil looked around the crowd gathered by the fire. 'Your family must be here. Everybody be here.' Her face turned serious. 'Nobody misses a full-moon selection. **It be the law**.'

Felix scanned the groups. The least he could do was *look* like he was searching for his family. Parents hugged their children close as the crackling fire cast moving shadows over their worried faces. The leopard group all wore spots of some sort on their clothing and the bears had little round ears on their furry hats. They looked like **supercool animal warriors**.

Felix studied their faces wondering what a 'full-moon selection' involved. Judging by how terrified they all seemed, it couldn't be good. As he scanned the crowd, stress filled each and every expression and –

Felix froze. His eyes stopped on a face. A familiar face. She had a bear hat pulled down over her head, but frizzy strands of hair still stuck out from underneath. Her wide, dark eyes darted around and Felix recognised something in them. It was the look of someone who didn't know where they were or what was going on, but was trying to figure it out.

Felix was very, **VERY** familiar with that feeling. She looked different in the leather and fur than she had in her unicorn onesie, but Felix was sure it was her. The girl from his last shower-teleporting adventure. The girl from the medieval town square. What was she doing ***here***?

Suddenly, her eyes locked on his. Her stare was intense and confused. Felix stood up to make his way over to her when –

BOOYAAAAAAAH!

The entire gathering rose to their feet, thrusting their fists in the air and cheering. Felix lost the girl in the crowd and was jammed between the others in the Fox clan. Through the bodies, he saw a woman walk over and climb onto a wooden structure built in front of the fire. It looked like a sort of scaffolding made from sticks, tied together with vine. At the top was a crude platform made from planks of wood. The lady looked down over the crowd, wearing a huge headdress made from twisted sticks woven with leaves.

She raised her hands and a hush fell over everyone. 'Bear, Fox and Leopard. We come together tonight on the full moon to find **the next Frivlig**. The pride of the mountains.'

Felix leant towards Torkal. 'What's a Frivlig?'

'The next person to face the yeti.'

'Ooooohhhhh.' Despite quite enjoying the way the word rolled around on his tongue, Felix was very happy to **not be a Frivlig**.

The woman with the twig-crown continued to speak and Felix went back to searching for the girl in the unicorn onesie . . . who technically wasn't in the onesie anymore. But with everyone on their feet she had disappeared into the mass of people.

The woman's voice continued to boom from the wooden podium. 'The full moon's Frivlig is the **revered hero** to our tri-villages. Although not one has returned successful thus far, when they do, they will be honoured by all for all time.'

Felix stood on his tippy-toes and tried to look for the girl between the people in the crowd. He caught a glimpse of the bear hat, but it disappeared again. Felix just couldn't keep track of her. There were too many bear hats. He once lost Olly at a Wiggles concert, which is the one place where having a kid in a bright yellow t-shirt is truly NOT helpful.

'And so, once again, under the light of the full moon, we ask for the brave Frivlig to **raise their hand**.'

Felix weaved between the fur covered bodies, heading towards the other group. He *had* to find this girl.

'Brave Frivlig, **show yourself!**'

A murmur rolled through the crowd as people shook their heads and slowly sat down.

Felix spotted her again. It was definitely her. How had she been in **both worlds?** It made no sense. But making no sense seemed to be Felix's jam right now, so the idea that he could maybe make no sense with someone else flooded him with a feeling of hope.

He raised his hand in the air and waved it frantically at her. 'Hey, you! Over there. Hi. It's me! The kid from the other world! **Remember?**' Felix suddenly became aware that everyone was staring at him and the crowd had gone dead silent in the cold night air.

'WE HAVE A FRIVLIG!' the lady on the podium announced.

The crowd roared and rose to their feet. People patted Felix on the back and shuffled him towards the front.

Felix twisted frantically and tried to dig his heels into the snow. But snow is slippery and he felt himself being pushed towards the podium. '**What?** No. I just … I wasn't …'

He tried to grab onto people but their fur coats just slipped through his grasp and the crowd cheered him on. 'I mean, I had my hand up, but not because I … **I'M NOT A FRIVLIG!**'

Too late. He'd put his hand up. He had been selected.

He was a Frivlig.

'I can't even go down Seashell Lane when Mrs Hasting's tabby cat is blocking the way. How am I going to get past a yeti!?'

But his protests were drowned out by the cheering of the tri-villagers.

'FRIVLIG! FRIVLIG! FRIVLIG!'

Chapter 8

Extremely inconvenient

The crowd pushed Felix up onto the podium.

He looked out over the villagers. Scanning each face, he found a mix of relief, concern and something that seemed to say, 'Boy, this kid is either silly-brave, or just plain silly.'

He spotted the girl. Felix hoped for a sign of encouragement, but instead she just shook her head at him and then planted her face in her hand.

Right then he knew **she must** be from his world, his time. Surely, facepalms were unique to his world, right?

The twig-crown woman wrapped her arm around Felix's shoulder and announced to the crowd: 'I, Pinhode, leader of the tri-villages, present to you our Frivlig.' She thrust Felix forward. 'Tonight, we send this brave young soul up the mountain to rid our people of the yeti who has terrorised our clans and stolen our children. May he be the first Frivlig to **SUCCEED!**'

The crowd roared.

Felix's gut churned like the time he ate a Cork Bay Cafe **Mega Monster Sundae** with extra chocolate topping, whipped cream and sprinkles on his seventh birthday. Just minutes before he spewed all over the back seat of his dad's Corolla. Which was just hours before they had a family car-cleaning session.

Pinhode turned to him and held him by the shoulders. 'What be your name, brave young Frivlig?'

'Felix,' he said quietly.

'What?'

'Felix!'

The crowd hushed and the woman's eyes widened.

'It's a sign!' she cried. 'A real-life Fearlax is our Frivlig!'

'Not Fearlax. Felix,' he tried to explain, but it was useless. The crowd was in a frenzy.

Felix could see how excited they all were. Here they had a new Frivlig ready and willing to face off with the yeti. AND he had the same name as their yeti-scarecrow. He might as well have been named **'Scare-Yeti'**. It was perfect. Well, for them anyway. It was extremely inconvenient for Felix, who had very little interest in hiking up a snow-covered mountain to face off against a kid-munching yeti.

'Hand me the helmet!' Pinhode cried, and a man passed her a very odd-looking hat. It was like a domed Viking helmet with antlers attached to the sides. She **plonked** it on Felix's head and fastened a leather strap under his chin. Felix tried to protest again, but it was no use. Things were on a roll and he was being swept along in what appeared to be a well-rehearsed process.

Yet another cloak was wrapped around him and Felix was bundled into a sleigh pulled by two snow-white wolves. Food and

weapons were piled in the back and before he knew what was happening, he was passed a set of reins attached to the wolves.

'Good luck, young Fearlax! May the moon's light guide your way.'

Felix tried one last time. 'I was actually just trying to get someone's attention and I –'

'HEE-YA!' Pinhode whipped the reins and sent the sleigh on its way.

'But I didn't ...' Felix called over his shoulder.

'Go forth, Frivlig. SLAY THE YETI AND **AVENGE THE CHILDREN!**'

As the wolves bounded up the mountain and the snow whipped against

Felix's face, he tried to work out how he felt. The best he could come up with was a bit . . . numb. But that could just be the cold. Or maybe he was getting used to this whole 'jumping into a new world and putting his life on the line for a complete stranger' thing? Nah, it was probably **the cold**.

He looked behind him and the bonfire faded into the distance. Was he really racing up a mountain to fight a yeti? **A YETI?** He wanted to pinch himself, but he couldn't really feel his fingers and wasn't entirely sure they were still there. Plus, he'd tried that 'maybe it's just a dream' thing and unfortunately, the shower world-jumping was all too real.

Chapter 9

Bernard the bear

The mountain grew steeper and the wolves slowed down. Felix took the opportunity to look behind him in the sleigh. He could see more blankets, some food, and a few weapons including a double-headed battleaxe. This was clearly going to be *very* helpful as Felix had used battleaxes many times defending himself against the **aggressive seagulls** at Cork Bay's Chip Shack.

Normally this kind of clever sarcasm would make Felix smile. But with no one to share it with, he was instead flooded with a sense of loneliness. Maybe that's why he'd wanted to get that girl's attention ***so much*** that he'd accidentally volunteered himself for what was, no doubt, a **death mission**. He'd seen her in both worlds. That had to mean something, right? That what was happening to him was happening to her? If he could find her, they could work out what was going on. Maybe even help each other. Assuming he wasn't dead by the end of this little adventure. Which he probably would be.

ROOOOAAAARRR!

The wolves skidded to a halt and the sleigh crashed into the back of them. Felix was catapulted over the front, tumbling through the dark and landing face first in the snow. He lifted his ice-covered head to see two massive paws in the powder in front of him. Raising his head, he saw that the paws were attached to the body of an enormous brown bear.

RAAAAAAAR! the bear roared, standing up on its hind legs, front paws ripping at the cold air. The wolves growled behind Felix, crouching down on their front legs. He seriously hoped they were up for defending him, but suspected if they weren't attached to a sleigh they would already be long gone.

Felix had thought his life would end at the hands of a yeti, but **being eaten** by a giant bear made sense too. He covered

his head with his arms (like that was going to help).

'Felix!'

It seemed weird that the bear knew his name. It should seem weird that the bear talked, but less and less surprised Felix these days. He peered up to see Torkal sitting on top of the bear, grinning down at him.

'Do not be scared. This be Bernard and he not be trying to bite your head off, that just be his way of saying **hello**.'

Felix carefully crawled to his feet and waved awkwardly at the bear. Bernard was now back on all fours and looking at Felix like he wouldn't even make a worthwhile appetiser.

'What are you doing here?' asked Felix.

Torkal slid down off the giant bear. 'I couldn't be letting you face the yeti alone, could I?' He patted the wolves. 'You don't **exactly** be looking up to the task.'

'What's that supposed to mean?'

Torkal kneeled and looked each of the wolves in the eyes. Their nerves after the bear encounter faded away

and they bowed their heads. Torkal gave each of them a gentle pat and they moved to the front of the sleigh, curling up on the ground.

He turned back to Felix. 'I'm not trying to be rude. But you don't really be seeming like the warrior type.'

Felix wanted to tell him that he was actually the **Year 5 thumb-wrestling champion** at Cork Bay PS, but he wasn't sure it would impress as much as he hoped.

'Plus,' Torkal continued, 'it might be helpful to have someone with you who can be talking to animals. Just in case you come across one who wants to be eating you?'

Felix couldn't really argue with that. 'Okay, sounds good. Thanks, Torkal.'

'Not a problem. Now what be the tactical plan?'

Felix laughed. 'There is no plan. As far as I can see, I'm being sent up a mountain to become a **yeti's shish kebab**.'

Torkal tilted his head. 'But if you don't have a plan, why did you be volunteering?'

'Now *that* is a long story.' Felix gathered himself up and collected the items that had been thrown from the sleigh. 'Maybe I can fill you in after we take down the yeti?'

'Excellent,' said Torkal, hurling himself up onto Bernard the bear. 'Let us go **find my brother!**'

Felix held onto the reins, but there was no pretending he was controlling the sleigh as it hurtled towards the mountain top. He was glad he wasn't alone on this mission. Torkal and his giant bear and his magic animal-speaking superpowers made Felix feel slightly better about the situation. He was still scared, but if he'd learnt anything from his experience of jumping into strange worlds (yes, **all two** of those times), it was that having company made things less overwhelming.

Last time, once Felix had solved the problem at hand, he'd been able to go home. He hoped it would be the same this time. He just **REALLY** wished the problem wasn't a hairy kid-eating mythical (or not-so-mythical) beast that lived in the freezing cold.

The sky was clear and crisp with stars that twinkled and seemed closer than he'd ever seen them. Snow-capped mountains surrounded Felix on all sides, glowing slightly in the moonlight.

For sure, it was weird and scary being thrown into random worlds, but it was also **pretty amazing**. When else would a kid from Cork Bay be racing through snowy mountains on a sleigh pulled by ice wolves? He and Olly had zoomed down the sand dunes on a bin lid once, but it really wasn't the same.

Felix had to appreciate the epic adventure.

That was until the **yeti's lair** came into view.

The sleigh reached the top of the mountain and the ice fog that clung to the mountain's peak started to clear. In the same way that big surf looks awesome until the giant wave is crashing down on your head, Felix's feelings towards his current situation shifted.

Still epic. But now also **terrifying**.

Chapter 10

Crucial for a successful extraction

Obviously, Felix had never seen a yeti's lair before. And this one did not disappoint. On top of the mountain, about a hundred metres in front of them, was a huge rock formation, standing like a jagged, stone pyramid, covered in ice and snow. At the front was a large opening with big icy spikes hanging from the top. If Olly had been there, he would have been able to tell Felix if they were stalactites or stalagmites. But Felix was just going to stick with **big, icy, spikey, hanging things**. It gave the impression that the entrance of the cave was a giant mouth.

Torkal and Bernard slowed down and moved behind a pile of large rocks on the outskirts of the cave. The wolves stopped next to the bear. Torkal and Felix crept up behind the rocks, peeking over at the scene before them.

'We will have to be leaving the sleigh and animals here,' whispered Torkal. 'We don't want the yeti to be seeing us approach.'

'Ah yes,' said Felix, trying to sound like this wasn't his first rescue mission. 'The element of surprise. Crucial for a **successful extraction**.'

Torkal looked at him like he'd been teleported from another world. Which was, well, fair. 'What?'

'Nothing. Sorry. Yes, no sleigh, no animals, sneaking, got it.'

'There be only one way in. This makes it tricky,' explained Torkal.

Felix was feeling unenthusiastic about walking into a giant cave mouth.

Maybe he could just keep lookout while Torkal went in and did the whole 'slay the yeti, rescue the kids' thing?

'You ready?' asked Torkal.

Or maybe not.

'Yep,' Felix lied.

'Turn your frakka the other way,' Torkal instructed as he removed his jacket.

'Why?' Felix asked, but followed his instructions.

Torkal pulled the layer back on, revealing the white fur inside. 'Because now we blend in. Making the snooking easier?'

Felix laughed as he pulled his own white fur over his head. 'The sneaking?

Yes, much easier. We will blend into the snow now. Okay, so camouflage done, what's the next move?'

Torkal frowned at Felix. 'It is you who be the Frivlig. You decide next move.'

'Ah yes,' Felix said nervously. 'About that . . .' Felix thought about what he would normally do in a situation like this. Minus the yeti and stolen children, of course.

Olly and Felix had snuck into an abandoned house in Cork Bay once because they'd heard there was a **possum with rabies** in there whose eyes glowed in the dark and it walked around on its hind legs like a person. What had he done then? Ah yes, what any smart big brother does.

Sent Olly in **first**.

Felix looked at Torkal. He was such a nice kid, it didn't seem fair. As he battled with his ethics, a squirrel scampered across the rock in front of him. It paused, shaking some flakes of snow from the top of its head. **That's it!**

'Torkal! We need to send in a scout. They can tell us what's going on inside before we head in.'

Torkal sighed. 'Fine! You big brothers really be all the same. If I don't come back, assume I be eaten and take over the mission, yas?' He got to his feet, but Felix yanked him back down behind the rock.

'Not you!' He pointed to the squirrel. **'Her!'**

The squirrel's head spun around and she stared at them wide-eyed with a look that said, 'How did I get sucked into this? I was just out on a nut hunt. Fight your own **yeti battles**.'

A grin spread across Torkal's face. 'Great idea!' He squatted down next to the squirrel and did his spooky animal eye-contact thing. They 'chatted' a bit until the squirrel crossed her little arms and tilted her head to the side.

Torkal turned to Felix. 'She wants something.'

'The squirrel is playing hardball? **Seriously?**'

Torkal shrugged. 'She'll do it. But she be wanting to know what's in it for her.'

'How about lifelong gratitude?' Felix replied sarcastically.

'I do not think squirrels really care about that. Got any **nuts?**'

Felix rolled his eyes. 'Of course I don't have any nu–' He stopped and slowly slid his hand into his pocket. His fingers wrapped around the **chestnuts** that he'd taken from the dinner table.

'You're not going to believe this but . . .' He pulled the nuts out and lay his palm out flat.

The squirrel nodded, leapt off the rocks and disappeared into the snow, bounding towards the cave's entrance.

'What now?' Felix asked.

'We wait.' Torkal pulled the sleigh up against the rocks and they both took a seat.

Ten minutes later, there was a soft scurrying on the rock behind them and Felix felt a light tap on his shoulder. He turned around to see the squirrel standing there with her little paw held out.

'**Info first**, then the nuts!' he demanded.

The squirrel sighed.

Felix didn't know squirrels could sigh. He didn't know they had this much attitude or drove such a hard bargain. Actually, he was starting to realise he didn't know much about squirrels at all.

Torkal put his head close to the furry creature and they 'spoke' for a while.

'What's she saying?' Felix asked after a couple of minutes of squirrel talk.

Torkal translated for Felix. 'She said it be very dark inside. When you go through the entrance, it opens out into an enormous cave. At the back of the cave there be a large cage. In the cage are giants.'

'Giants!' Felix cried. 'Just in case yetis weren't **bad enough**.'

Torkal shook his head. 'She said "giants like us". So I'm guessing she be actually meaning kids.'

'Squirrel perspective. I guess.' Felix shrugged. 'So that means they're all alive?'

Torkal nodded. 'Certainly some of them are. I asked how many kids but apparently squirrels can't count.'

'And the yeti?'

'She didn't see it, but she be hearing some noises coming from the back of the cave. A sort of **crunching sound**. Like the sound of human bones being put through a grinder.'

Felix stared at the squirrel. 'How in SpongeBob does she know what **THAT** sounds like?'

Torkal shook his head. 'No idea. Squirrels can be kind of **creepy**.'

Felix gave the squirrel a side eye which the furry creature completely ignored.

'Anything else?' asked Felix.

The squirrel nattered away for a bit and then Torkal translated. 'She said **try not to get eaten**.'

'Solid advice,' Felix muttered and handed the chestnuts to the squirrel.

She snatched them out of his hand, whispered something to Torkal and scampered away.

'What was that last thing?' asked Felix.

Torkal grinned. 'She said it be okay if **YOU** get eaten.'

Felix glared at the squirrel as it paused on the rock and sneered at him. 'Harsh burn from a **squirrel**.'

Chapter 11

Be the bait

Felix felt more confident now that they knew what they were up against. The fact that what they were up against was a giant, furry, bone-crunching snow beast made things less cheerful. But at least

Felix felt like he was moving forward. This was surely his way of getting home. Save the kids, happy families back together and **ZAP!** He'd be back in his shower at home with his weird dad waiting for him to finish. And he should make it home in time for his trip to the zoo. He just had to **avoid getting eaten** (as previously pointed out by a squirrel).

'I have an idea,' said Torkal.

'Great!' Felix was relieved. 'Cos' I don't.'

'You go up to the cave. I be going to lure the yeti out. When I do, run in, release the kids and get out as fast as you can.'

'Lure the yeti out? With what?' asked Felix.

Torkal gave him a wicked smile. 'Bait!'

Felix didn't like the sound of that. 'What kind of bait?'

'The one thing we know it likes – **a small human!**'

'Do you mean . . .'

Torkal puffed his chest out proudly. 'Yes, me! **I be the bait**.'

'Did you not hear what the squirrel said?'

'Don't worry about me,' explained Torkal. 'You just be getting the kids free. Come, let us go.'

Torkal collected some things from the sleigh and slung them over his shoulder. Felix followed his lead and grabbed a knapsack, throwing it on his back. The boys trudged through the snow towards the yeti's cave.

When they reached the entrance, they couldn't see anything but a big black hole.

'Next time I really need to pack a torch,' said Felix. 'And maybe some clothes and food . . . and yeti repellent.' But all those things were **pretty hard** to fit in a pair of speedos.

'I think I can help.' Torkal raised his head and whistled into the night sky. Felix heard a soft hum. A small cloud of insects flew towards them, buzzing just over Torkal's head. He 'spoke' to them for a second and then they moved away and hovered over Felix instead.

He looked at Torkal, confused. 'Where I come from, being followed around by a **bunch of blowflies** is not something you ask for. How is this going to help?'

'Like this!' Torkal clicked his fingers and the swarm lit up, glowing like a soft night-light. 'These be not blowflies. These be fireflies.'

'Cooooooo!!' Felix walked forward a bit and the swarm followed him, lighting his path.

Torkal adjusted the ropes and gear on his shoulder. 'Turn them off, go and hide by the cave mouth. I'll draw the yeti out. Once it be outside, go in, turn the flies on and find the children. Got it?'

'Sure. Sounds simple enough.' Felix regretted his sarcasm instantly because he certainly wasn't contributing to the plan and definitely didn't have a **better idea**. He clicked his fingers and the flies turned off. Hiding behind a rock at the mouth of the cave, he waited there like instructed.

Torkal made his way over to a large tree. He carefully removed the gear from his shoulder. Walking around the tree, he lay objects out and adjusted bits and pieces. He was quite far away and through the soft snow that still fell silently, Felix couldn't see exactly what he was doing.

Torkal then raised his hands to his mouth and made a strange-sounding call.

'Ooo Ooooohhh. **Ooo Ooooohhh**.'

Seconds later, a black shape swooped past the tree, circled around once and landed next to Torkal. The scene played out before Felix like a shadow puppet performance. The two silhouettes, one bird, one boy, stood together discussing something. Finally, Torkal handed over an object, and with a flap of its wings, the bird disappeared up into the tree.

Torkal stepped out in front of the cave, standing tall and shoulders back.

Felix guessed this was probably the 'bait' part of the plan and he couldn't help but wonder whether Torkal knew quite how to get a yeti's attention.

'Salutations, yeti!' Torkal yelled into the darkness of the cave.

'Well, that'll probably do it,' whispered Felix to himself.

'I be a child. Um, a small, defenceless child, out here, just hanging around. Doing nothing. No adults to protect me. You might be wanting to come out and, um, be snatching me ... for your **bone crunching**.'

Felix cringed. 'That's probably overdoing it.' But then he heard movement coming from the cave – it had worked!

Torkal stood his ground, feet planted firmly in the snow. A shadow stretched outside and darkness fell over him. Footsteps **crunched** in the snow as a huge shape followed the shadow.

Felix stopped breathing for a second as the giant hairy creature ducked its head to step through the mouth of the cave. He'd seen yetis in books, drawings, blurry photos of people who'd claimed to have spotted them and, of course, in cartoons and movies, but this was **something else**.

The yeti must have been over five metres tall. That's like three of Felix's dad standing on each other's shoulders (with an Olly on top for good measure).

But *that* still would have been a very tall bunch of skinny people. And there was **nothing** skinny about the yeti. It was the Dwayne 'The Rock' Johnson of yetis. Huge shoulders and chest, giant hands with thick sausage-like fingers and a big pear-shaped head. Like, even bigger than Olly's head when he was a toddler. Its mouth was full of sharp, yellow teeth (perfect for munching on small children) and its **entire body** was covered with thick white fur, the ends slightly frosted with snow.

It spotted Torkal and slowly approached the boy. As it stood in front of him, towering over the kid like a furry skyscraper, Felix felt like a coward. How could he hide behind a rock and

watch his new friend become a child sushi platter?

He whipped off his backpack and dug through the contents, hoping for a **high-powered drone** decked out with lasers. Unfortunately, the best he found was a homemade slingshot.

'Really,' Felix groaned. 'What kind of adult packed this useless survival kit?'

Since it was all he had to work with, Felix searched around desperately for something to load the slingshot. His hand landed on a small rock which he tucked into the pocket of the weapon. But as he pulled back to take aim, he realised it was all too little (like, **waaaaaay** too little) and definitely too late.

'You hungry?' Torkal teased the yeti. He strutted back and forth in front of the huge creature like he was on a fashion show catwalk. 'Look at me, I be **delicious**. One hundred per cent premium kid bones here, all for the taking.'

The yeti tilted its head to the side, confused. Felix didn't blame it, Torkal looked ridiculous. Almost as ridiculous as Felix did about to shoot a five-metre-tall **abominable snowman** with a sling-shotted rock. It would be like throwing a peanut at a bulldozer.

But unlike Felix, Torkal wasn't giving up.

'This be a one-time offer. Bones perfect for crunching. Don't miss out.'

Torkal's sales pitch was clearly too good. The yeti reached a giant hand towards him, but he ducked to the side and ran to the tree. Scampering like a monkey, Torkal began to climb. The yeti swiped at him but it was **way slower** than Torkal, so he ducked and avoided the yeti's hands again.

The yeti leant against the tree, swinging at the boy with its giant monster paws. Suddenly, a shape swooped past its head, circled around the tree and past again. Then another, and another. Something trailed behind the shapes and the yeti turned to swipe at them. Felix squinted in the dark, peering through the light snow.

'Owls!'

The birds were white owls and clutched in their claws were ropes. They circled the tree in opposite directions, ducking and weaving as they passed each other. The ropes wrapped around the tree, and more importantly, around the yeti. Before it even knew what was happening, the hairy creature was strapped to the tree. Just like when Felix tied Olly to the telephone pole during their games of cops and robbers.

Tied up and going **nowhere**.

Felix knew it was his turn. He checked that the fireflies were still hovering overhead and moved towards the mouth of the cave. Standing at the entrance for

a moment, he peered into the darkness. It was pitch black and **eerily quiet**. He paused for a moment, surprised by how brave he was being. Usually, he was the one to make Olly catch the cockroaches and take them outside. Yet here he was, facing off against a giant yeti to save a bunch of kids. Okay, so maybe Torkal was the one actually facing off with the yeti. But Felix was helping, which is more than he ever did with the cockroaches.

Perhaps being in a strange land gave him courage, or maybe somewhere deep down he still thought it might be a dream. And it's easy to be brave in a dream. Either way, he was **pretty impressed with himself**.

Felix pulled his shoulders back, clicked his fingers and with the fireflies lighting his way, he stepped **bravely** into the cave.

Chapter 12

Red-tongue lizard girl

Inside the cave, it was exactly how the squirrel had described. The entrance led into a small tunnel and then quickly opened out. The space was big enough for the yeti to have plenty of head room.

The fireflies' light wasn't enough to illuminate much of the space, so Felix moved slowly around, revealing details as he went. There was a large fire-pit with a giant pot resting in the middle. Probably for making **kid-stew**. Crude-looking utensils hung high up on the walls and a sort of nest lay in the corner. But Felix wasn't here to inspect the place for a home makeover. He had **one mission**, and the squirrel said the kids were in a cage at the back of the cave.

He moved deeper into the giant grotto. A slurping sound echoed from the depths. But not just one sound ... many. Like lots of creatures slurping on milkshakes. What if there were more yetis? A whole family of them? **A whole football team?** And they had just made up a batch of kid eyeball milkshakes?

Felix didn't feel quite as brave as he had a few moments ago when he thought the only yeti around was safely detained by some cool ninja owls. But he had no choice. If he wanted to get home, he had to save the kids.

Pushing himself forward, Felix reached the bars of the cage. The slurping was now louder, but Felix couldn't see more than a metre in front of him.

He looked up at the flies. 'Go! Over there. Please, flies.' But he clearly

didn't speak firefly. He really needed Torkal. 'Light. There,' he said, pointing dramatically. As his hands swept past, the flies moved a little but then regrouped. 'Well, maybe fireflies work the same as blowflies back home.' Felix waved his hands around frantically. **'Shoo flies, shoo!'** The fireflies spread, flying out into the cave and lighting up the large space.

Felix stared at the scene in front of him.

There, in the cage, were **the kids**.

But they weren't thin and terrified and awaiting his heroic rescue like Felix had expected. They were well fed, and rugged up nice and warm, and pretty happy looking.

The kids were surrounded by toys and games and carefully built climbing equipment with slides and swings. Way cooler ones than you would ever find in a playground back home where adults are more worried about kids not getting hurt than they are about them **actually having any fun**. Here there were rings on ropes, swinging over ponds and giant climbing structures. It was more like a **ninja warrior** course than boring play equipment.

One kid in a fox hood rubbed his hands together and a little ball of fire was created. He placed it gently on the ground where it continued to burn as some other kids gathered around.

Felix guessed it must have been her Rising. He immediately wished Risings were a thing back in Cork Bay. The kids at school would be seriously impressed if he could just casually move a mountain or something.

Some kids were snuggled up in a bed or a cot, hugging **little yeti teddies** and looking perfectly content.

And every single one of them was slurping on a **snow cone**.

'Who are you?' asked one small kid, her lips blue, not from cold but from the flavouring on her icy treat.

'Um, I'm Felix. I've come to rescue you from the **terrifying yeti** and take you back to your families.'

The kid shrugged. 'I suppose. But can I be getting one more snow cone first?'

'If we go home,' another boy called out from the hammock he sat in, 'do we be getting to come back here to play?'

Felix shook his head in confusion. 'Um, I don't know. I hadn't really thought ... um, let me ask Torkal.'

'You know Torkal?' said a voice.

Felix looked up as a tall boy swung down from a thick rope and dropped onto a platform.

He zipped down a slide and landed in front of Felix. 'How is he? **Where is he?**'

The resemblance was clear. This kid was a taller, broader and slightly cheekier-looking version of Torkal.

'Sten?' Felix asked.

'Yas!' Sten's eyes lit up in the low light.

Felix grinned back. 'He's just outside. With the yeti. I mean not hanging out with the yeti, but you know, he's got it trapped and held hostage.'

'Oh no!' A small girl stepped towards the bars of the cage holding a red snow cone and licking

furiously between words. 'He hasn't **slurp** hurt her **slurp** has he **slurp?**' She must have had raspberry flavour because her little tongue that flicked in and out like a thirsty lizard was bright red.

'Hurt who? Who's her?'

'Myrtle.' A boy about the same age as Olly stepped forward. He wasn't holding a snow cone, but lime was clearly his choice of flavour because his lips were an Oscar the Grouch green. 'Myrtle be the yeti. She's the best.'

'The best?' Felix was seriously confused. 'Didn't she kidnap you all?'

Sten nodded his head to the side. 'Well, technically yes.'

'And lock you up in this cage?'

'Also true. **Slurp**,' agreed red-tongued lizard girl.

'And eat you and grind your bones up!'

'What?' cried the green-lipped kid. 'She would never be doing that!'

Sten reached through the bars and grabbed Felix's arm. 'We all be fine. Myrtle be taking good care of us and the only grinding going on be the endless production of snow cones she be making for us.'

A voice came from the corner of the cave. 'Every flavour you can imagine. And no limits on refills.' A girl wearing a coat with a big furry hood stood at a huge machine, turning the handle. As the crushed ice tumbled into the cone she held underneath, Felix recognised the sound it made.

The sound of **human bones** being put through a grinder.

Or, as it turned out, an all-you-can-eat **snow cone buffet**.

Felix knew he shouldn't have trusted that squirrel with an attitude.

The girl stopped churning the ice and held the frozen ball up to Felix.

'Want one?' she asked with a grin.

Chapter 13

She is not an it

Felix knew he shouldn't waste time eating snow cones. He had a job to do. Rescue these kids from this terrible situation (which turned out to be not so terrible, but ... details!) so he can get home.

But he **did** like snow cones. Especially pineapple flavoured. And these kids didn't seem to be in a hurry. And his dad always said it was rude to say no when someone offered you a snow cone. Well, not specifically a snow cone, but close enough.

'Yeah, okay. Pineapple please.'

The girl grabbed a bottle from the shelf and squeezed yellow syrup all over the cone. **'One pineapple coming up!'**

Felix did wonder how many pineapples there were growing in the snowy mountains but decided not to question it.

He turned back to Sten. 'So, you guys are . . . okay?'

'Ah yas. We be having a great time. Playing all day, snow cones all night, no school. And Myrtle has being very kind to us.'

By now the excitement (and the fireflies) had all the kids out of bed. Felix could see how happy they were, playing games and slurping down icy treats.

The girl passed Felix's snow cone through the bars and he took a bite. It was outrageously delicious. There may not be any pineapples in the mountains, but the flavour was spot-on. 'Really? So you've just been **chillin' out** having a good time?'

The girl nodded. 'I think Myrtle is just lonely. She be needing some friends. She didn't want to hurt us.'

'Yeah, well, I don't think good friends **keep their friends in cages**, no matter how many snow cones they feed you. Don't you miss your families?' Felix asked.

Sten's smile fell. 'I do. We do. That be true.'

'Okay. Then it's time to get you home. Because they are all **VERY** worried about you and miss you heaps and I really need to get home.' Felix looked around the cage and noticed a big lock on the door. 'There!' he pointed. 'Where is the key?'

Sten sighed. 'Yah, good luck with that.' He pointed high up on the wall where a giant iron key hung on a rusty nail. It would have been about chest height for the yeti which meant it was about giraffe height for Felix. There was **no way** he could reach it.

Felix looked around. 'There's got to be something useful around here. What kind of stuff did the yeti use? Weapons, torture devices, poking sticks?'

Sten's face screwed up. '**What? No! Myrtle would never**.'

'Right. Friendly, snow cone yeti. Got it. Well, I need something.' Felix patted his body and his hand landed on something sticking out of his pocket.

The slingshot! Perfect.

'Now I just need a rock or something.' Felix hunted around on the floor but it was icy and smooth.

Oscar the Grouch-lipped kid pointed to the corner of the cave and smiled. 'There be something over there you could probably use.'

Felix walked over to where he was pointing. There, in the corner, lay a small pile of black pellets. Perfect for sling-shotting. Felix picked one up and rolled it around in his fingers. 'What is it?'

'Frozen fox poo!'

'Eeeeeeewwwww!' Felix dropped the pellet, wiping his hands on his pants. 'Does anyone have a wet wipe?'

'A what?' asked Sten.

Felix sighed. 'Never mind.' He stared at the fox poop. There wasn't a lot of choice. He had to get the key and he need ammo. Felix reminded himself it was all in the name of getting home. So he screwed up his nose, bent down and grabbed a handful of **poop-ammo**.

Felix went back to where the key was hanging and carefully loaded his slingshot. Ready, aim, **fire!** His first shot hit the key but it didn't budge.

'Shoot from the side.'

'Use more poo!'

'Aim from underneath.'

By now all the kids were lined up along the bars, yelling unwanted advice. It was like when Felix played Mario Bros and Olly would **NOT** stop yelling 'get the coins!'. But times about twenty.

Felix blocked it all out and focused. Eight years with Olly had made him a professional at blocking things out. He aimed at the bottom of the key, pulled back on his poop pellet and fired slightly from the side.

It was perfect!

The key flicked up, tossing the ring sideways and flinging it off the rusty nail.

CLANG! The key hit the icy floor and skidded towards Felix. The kids cheered. Despite the snow cones, these kids were ready to go home.

RAAAAAOOOOOOWWWW!

A yeti roar came from outside the cave.

'Quick,' Sten whispered. 'Unlock the door.'

Felix picked up the huge key and stood on his tippy-toes, trying to reach the lock, but it was too high.

'Pass it here.' Sten grabbed the key and turned to the kids. **'Stacks on!'** The biggest kid of the group stood under the lock and held the bars of the cage tightly. Taking a run-up, Sten placed one foot on the kid's calf and sprung onto his back. It sort of looked like a specky in the AFL, but instead of crashing to the ground, Sten stayed on his shoulders.

'Here I come!' A small girl swung across the rings, flying through the air like Spider-Man and landing, less than gracefully, on top of Sten. She scrambled to her feet and Sten passed her the key which she slid into the lock and turned.

'WE BE FREEEEEE!' the kids cried as they pushed the door open.

RAAAAARRRRRGGGGHHHH!

The yeti's cries were sounding more desperate.

Torkal appeared at the entrance of the cave. 'I don't know how much longer those ropes will hold it. We have got to go ... **NOW!**'

'Torkal!' Sten cried and ran to his brother, swallowing him up in a massive hug.

Felix joined them. 'Emotional family reunions and healthy displays of brotherly love will have to wait. **Run!**'

They turned and bolted from the cave, the rest of the kids following behind.

As they ran out into the night, there was the yeti. Still bound to the tree, but definitely close to breaking free from the ropes.

'Move!' yelled Torkal as they ran towards the big rock they were originally hiding behind. The wolves were still waiting with the sleigh but looked very nervous about the angry yeti nearby. Huddling there, they waited for all the kids to catch up.

Felix peeked over the rock. The ropes around the yeti were straining to the point of breaking. They weren't going to hold for much longer.

'What now?' Felix asked Torkal. 'Everyone won't fit in the sleigh and we can't walk all the way back to the village. The yeti is almost free. It will catch up with us for sure.'

'She be not an it,' corrected a little girl. **'Her name be Myrtle.'**

'Don't worry.' Torkal smiled. 'As always, I be having a plan.' He whistled into the night sky.

Felix heard the sound of footsteps crunching in the snow and then out of the trees appeared an **entourage of animals**: deer, moose, bears, arctic hares, wolves and snow leopards.

'Coooooooool!' Felix whispered.

'Everyone choose an animal. Small kids, on the smaller ones please. Jump on and hold on tight.' Torkal grinned at his

brother who had climbed up onto a large deer. 'We be going home.'

RRRAAAAAAARRRRR!

From behind the kids came a huge **snap** as the yeti tore free from the ropes that held her.

'Hee-ya!' Torkal cried as the army of animals, with children on their backs, bolted through the thick snow and down the mountain.

Towards their homes.

And their families.

Chapter 14

Ice-atarian

Felix clung to the fur of the moose he was riding, the snow stinging his face. He let that sink in for a moment. A few hours ago, he was showering in his speedos in Cork Bay and now he was galloping down a snowy mountain on a **moose** being chased by a **yeti**.

His life had really taken a turn.

Felix looked over his shoulder, trying not to slip off the moose's back. It didn't look like the yeti was chasing them, so that was good news.

But Felix had a weird feeling in the bottom of his tummy.

Soon he would get all the kids back to their parents. Then he'd get zapped back to his home like nothing had happened. He knew it would be just like it had been last time. The story of his adventure would burn away inside him but he couldn't tell anyone. **Who would believe him?**

The last couple of weeks had been hard. Felix had tried to pretend the first adventure hadn't happened, that it was all a dream.

But now he knew better.

He wanted **so bad** to tell his dad, his friends, even Olly. But no one would understand. *He* didn't even really understand.

'There!' Sten yelled from his deer.

Ahead, through the dark and the snow, came the soft glow of the village fire. The kids would be home soon. Which meant Felix would be too.

The army of animals with their kid-passengers galloped into the village, arriving at the bonfire where the tri-villagers still waited. The kids slid from their steeds and ran to their families.

'Sten! Torkal!' Norg and Bodil cried as the boys sprinted into their arms. They disappeared into a giant furry-jacket embrace.

Felix slowly slid off his moose, gave it a thank-you pat and stood in the snow, watching the reunions.

That little homesick feeling swirled around inside him and his eyes welled up just a pinch.

Felix was the first to admit he'd often cry in a decent tear-jerker movie. That wildebeest bit in *The Lion King* got him every time (you know the bit). And he was a **blubbering mess** by the end of literally EVERY Pixar movie. So big family reunions when he was far from home and missing his own family were always going to turn on the waterworks.

'You did it!' Norg cried, moving to Felix. 'You be saving our children!' He wrapped an arm around Felix and turned to the crowd. 'Three booyah for the Fearlax!'

'BOOYAH!' the crowd cheered.

'BOOYAH!'

'BOOYAAAH!'

Felix beamed back. 'Well, thanks, everyone. But I couldn't have done it without Torkal. I mean literally. I'm not just being modest here. Ninety per cent of the plan was his. He faced off with the yeti. He organised the band of animals to bring the kids safely home. Pretty much all I did was a roughly accurate shot with a piece of **frozen fox poop**.'

The crowd stared at him, blinking in silence.

'A fourth booyah for the Fearlax!'

'BOOYAAAAAAAH!'

Felix shrugged at Torkal who just laughed and gave his family another hug. It seemed having his brother back was enough of a reward for him.

Norg grinned at Felix. 'Now you stay with us? Live here. We make you third son.'

Felix smiled at their kindness. 'Oh no. I mean, thank you but I'm about to **zap off** at any second. Try not to be too frightened when I do. It's sort of like magic but good magic I promise.'

Norg's brow furrowed. 'Zap off?'

'Yes. Disappear, vanish, teleport. It's about to happen.'

The villagers gathered around, staring at Felix.

‘Did yeti hit you on the head?’ Bodil asked, a little concerned.

Felix looked between the villagers. All the kids were with their parents. Sten was back where he belonged.

Problem solved. **So why wasn’t he zapping?**

‘Any second now,’ he said, trying to convince himself as much as the villagers.

Nothing.

‘Any … second …’

Still nothing.

‘Maybe I need to say a magic word or something?’ Felix tried to think of his last moments in the previous world. Had he said something special?

'Problem solved!' he announced dramatically.

Nothing.

'My work here is done!'

Nope.

'There's no place like home!'

Clear plagiarism.

'Are you okay?' asked Torkal.

Felix shook his head. 'I don't get it. I saved you all, you're home with your families. I should zap back now. But it's not working. What if I'm stuck here?'

'Eeeeeeeeekkkkkkk!'

A loud scream came from the crowd as the villagers turned and drew their weapons. Heavy footsteps came down the mountain. Moving slowly towards them. Then out of the snowy mist stepped ... the yeti! Not roaring or running but walking slowly, almost sadly.

The adult villagers brandished their weapons.

'ATTACK!'

But as they charged at the yeti, the kids ran to form a barrier around her.

'STOP!' yelled Sten.

'Don't hurt her,' cried red-tongue lizard girl.

'Leave Myrtle alone!'

The adults froze, shocked to see their children protecting their captor.

Felix saw a figure step out from behind the yeti. He moved closer.

It was **her!**

The girl. The unicorn-onesie girl. She stared straight at Felix and then pointed to the yeti.

Felix had no idea what she wanted. Did she want him to fight the yeti? Because that was **NOT** going to happen. He looked at her, confused.

She rolled her eyes and tried again. Pointing to all the kids and families around her, she gave a thumbs up. But then she pointed to the yeti again and made a sad face.

Did she want him to help the yeti?

He grabbed Torkal. 'Can you talk to the yeti? Like how you can talk to animals?'

He shrugged. 'I never tried.'

'You should,' Felix suggested.

They walked over to where the yeti stood behind the army of kids. Felix waved Myrtle down and the giant creature crouched in the snow.

Torkal tried talking to her and the yeti growled back. He smiled and nodded at Felix. 'I be understanding her!'

Unicorn-onesie girl was **RIGHT THERE**! Felix tried to get her attention, but some of the Bear villagers gathered around her.

'Everybody stop!' Torkal announced. 'Myrtle has **something to say**.'

Torkal sat in the yeti's hand and she carefully lifted him up to the wooden podium where Pinhode had stood before in her twig-crown.

The villagers watched, ready to attack should the yeti decide to suddenly pop Torkal in her mouth like a gummy bear.

'Myrtle would like to apologise for stealing your children.'

The yeti leant in and whispered something to Torkal.

'Sorry, would like to apologise for ***borrowing*** your children. She never had any intention of hurting them and she be taking very good care of them while they were with her.'

'It be true,' shouted one kid. **'Best snow cones ever!'**

All the kids cheered.

The yeti spoke again and Torkal translated. 'It gets very lonely up there on the mountain and she never be getting invited to any of our village parties.'

'To be fair,' yelled one of the parents, 'they usually be meetings discussing the best way to hunt down and destroy the yeti. If we be inviting her ... **little awkward**, no?'

Torkal translated and responded.

'She understands that and agrees that her approach was not the best. She just thinks humans be beautiful and intriguing and wanted to be able to look at them whenever she pleased. But they ... we ... tend to run away.'

'So what do we do?' Someone yelled from the crowd.

Felix had once had a bunch of friends for a sleepover and Olly had behaved like an **absolute brat**. Until Dad suggested they just include him. Once they did, he immediately stopped throwing Maltesers at them from the kitchen and running in front of the TV with his undies on his head.

If it worked for little brothers, maybe it would work for **giant yetis**.

Felix tugged on the creature's ankle fur and pointed to the podium. The yeti bent down and lifted him to join Torkal.

'It seems pretty straightforward to me,' Felix called to the crowd. '**Include Myrtle**. Invite her to the bonfire parties. Perhaps discuss something other than her destruction. Then maybe she could make friends instead of being tempted to kidnap people? And in return, she could let you come to the forest to collect the wood you need to build and fix your houses?'

The villagers murmured between themselves and Torkal spoke to the yeti.

Torkal turned to the crowd. 'Myrtle agrees. She even said she could be helping bring the wood to us so we don't be having to cart it down the mountain.'

'Wait!' called one of the men in the fox-ear hats. 'We can't be making an agreement with this monster. **It stole our children.** And slaughtered every Frivlig we sent before the Fearlax. It cannot be trusted.'

'Whoa, whoa, **whoa!**' yelled the red-tongue lizard girl. 'For the last time, not "it"... "she". And *she* prefers to go by Myrtle. AND those Frivligs **are not dead**.' She pointed up the mountain. 'All the adults be up there, safe and sound. Myrtle collected them in a little cave and took care of them too. Just no snow cones for them.'

Felix turned on her, wide-eyed. 'Um, you didn't think to mention that? I mean we could have brought them down too, you know?'

The girl shrugged. 'I figured we could get them later. Plus, there was all the excitement with the great escape and the riding animals. **Adults are easy to forget**.'

Felix took a deep breath and shook his head, turning back to the crowd. 'The point is, no one got hurt and I think we can find a way for everyone to live in harmony.' He waved his hand over the crowd in front of him. 'You get the wood you need and Myrtle gets some company.'

Pinhode returned to the podium. 'And she promises **not to eat anyone?**'

Torkal checked. 'She actually be an **ice-atarian**. Snow cones only. So that shouldn't be a problem.'

'Very well. Bear, Fox and Leopard, do we have an agreement? Can the tri-villagers and this yeti live in harmony?'

Torkal whispered to Pinhode.

'I'm sorry. Can the tri-villagers and **Myrtle** live in harmony?'

The crowd murmured.

Felix groaned. 'This is where you all agree because the only alternative is living your lives in fear of someone who isn't to be feared.'

Still the villagers seemed unsure.

Torkal whispered to him.

'Really?' said Felix. 'That will work?'

Torkal shrugged. 'They are adults.'

Felix sighed and in his most dramatic voice announced:

'THE FEARLAX COMMANDS YOU!'

And it worked.

The adults cheered in agreement and Pinhode shook hands with Myrtle.

Felix searched for the unicorn-onesie girl and found her among the crowd. They locked eyes.

He wanted to get to her. He needed to know where she had come from. But as he made his move, she gave him a small sideways smile and waved goodbye.

REEEEKKKKKK!

The sound of rusty brakes ... a flash of white light ... the smell of singed hair.

Chapter 15

The inevitable

The water hit the fur jacket Felix was wearing and the drops bounced off like tiny tennis balls.

'How you going in there, buddy? Clean as a whistle yet?'

The sound of his dad's voice warmed Felix inside. Or maybe it was the ten layers of winter clothing plus the hot shower water in a Cork Bay summer.

'Almost, Dad,' said Felix as he tried to strip off the layers of clothes Norg had given him. 'Just getting behind those ears.'

'That's my boy. I really don't know why you've avoided the shower for so long. There's nothing better than an early morning scrub. Puts the **zing in your step**, I reckon.'

'You bet.' Felix piled the clothes up in the corner of the shower, adding to the fur mountain until he was back down to his speedos. He had to admit he did feel kind of gross. Dad was sure to check, so he grabbed the soap and gave himself a wash while he was in there ... he was hopefully done with zapping for the day.

He rinsed the smell of moose off his body and shampooed the scent of yeti from his hair. By the end, he could have sworn he was **actually sparkling** like a previously grubby t-shirt in a laundry detergent commercial.

Felix turned off the shower and dramatically pulled back the curtain.

'Ta da!'

Dad grinned at him. 'Look at you! I knew my beautiful son was somewhere there under all those layers of grime.' He snatched a fluffy towel from the rail and wrapped it around Felix, turning him into a cosy human sausage roll. Dad stayed there hugging his son for a minute, then stepped back.

'You know I love you clean or dirty, right? But **showers are non-negotiable** in this house, okay?'

Felix wished his dad really knew what that meant for him. But instead, he just nodded.

Dad smiled. 'All right, now let's get you ready for that zoo trip, huh?'

He went to leave but Felix grabbed his arm. 'Dad, I don't think I want to go to the zoo.'

'What?' Dad was puzzled. 'But you've been looking forward to this for ages. You love animals.'

'Right,' Felix agreed. 'But I don't think that you should put something you love in cages. What about all those animals' families? I bet they miss them. I'd miss you.'

Dad pulled Felix to him, giving him a squeeze. 'Aw, buddy, I'd miss you too if . . . you were . . . **in a cage**.'

Felix wanted to laugh. He knew Dad was trying to be supportive, but also

probably thought his son was watching too many horror movies or something.

'How about we go to the **dog shelter** instead?' Felix suggested. 'We could take a few of the dogs for a walk, play fetch with them, make a bit of a day of it?'

Dad nodded slowly. 'You know what, I don't have a job until this arvo. I was just going to do some admin this morning sooooo ... sure, **why not!**'

He let go of Felix and walked to the door. 'You get dressed and I'll get Olly to school, then we can head in.'

'Maybe Olly could come too?'

Dad looked at Felix like he had suggested they dress Olly in feathers and make him **do the samba**. 'Really?'

'Yeah, as a family.'

Dad's head tilted slightly and a smile crawled onto his lips. 'Okay, then maybe I'll try to move that arvo job and we could go for ice cream after. What do you reckon?'

Felix grinned. 'I could go for a **snow cone**.'

'Snow cones it is.' Dad left the bathroom, pulling the door behind him. But just before it closed, he paused. 'This whole dog shelter visit is not a ploy to get a **pet dog**, is it? Because the answer is **still no**.'

Felix shook his head. 'Promise, Dad. Just thought it would be nice. For us and the dogs.'

'All righty. Then get ready and meet me in the kitchen. **Family day!**'

Dad finally left and Felix was alone in the bathroom. He pulled back the curtain and stared at the soggy pile of mountain clothes stacked in the corner. Opening the small window next to the shower, he stuffed them out one by one, figuring he could go around the side of the house and deal with them later.

When the last boot was out, he leant on the sink. The mirror was fogged up so he wiped his towel across it, revealing his clean face. Felix stared at his reflection. He somehow looked older. Like all this **adventuring** was making him grow up.

It felt good to be home. But if this was going to keep happening – and **all signs pointed to yes** – he had to figure out how to work with it.

Find the problem, solve the problem, **zap home**.

Was it really that simple? And why was it happening to ***him*?**

But it wasn't just him was it?

The girl!

Felix closed his eyes and remembered the last moments before he zapped back. Seeing her face.

The knowing smile. The little wave goodbye. Maybe she knew something he didn't.

Next time, he would **HAVE** to talk to her.

Next time.

Felix was beginning to understand.

A 'next time' was inevitable.

HAVE YOU READ FELIX'S FIRST ADVENTURE IN SHOWER LAND?

Felix hates Mondays. Dad's yelling at him to get up. His little brother, Olly, is being super annoying. So when Felix shuts the bathroom door, he wishes he could get away. He turns on the shower and …

REEEEKKKKKK!

Felix finds himself standing in the middle of a field … naked … with an army of soldiers charging at him.

Step 1: **Avoid flying pitchforks!**

Step 2: Find some **PANTS**.

Step 3: **UM, IS THAT A DRAGON?!**

WAIT UNTIL YOU SEE WHAT HAPPENS NEXT!

Felix's shower is a portal to another world. Never fear. He's ready for anything this time, with a backpack full of survival gear. He turns on the shower and ...

REEEEKKKKKK!

Felix finds himself in the middle of the ocean ... sinking ... but there's a ship on the horizon.

Step 1: **Don't drown.**

Step 2: **Don't think about sharks.**

Step 3: **WHO IS THAT MYSTERY GIRL?**

In Shower Land: Break the Curse, *Nat and James wrote biographies for each other. For this book, they have decided to draw portraits of each other.*

Before judging the following artwork, please remember that one of these people is a professional illustrator with years of experience and tons of talent. And the other ... is Nat.